THE LOST ELEPHANT
AND THE SOUL TREE

THE LOST ELEPHANT AND THE SOUL TREE

AKILA KANNADASAN

ILLUSTRATED BY ENAKSHI GOSWAMI

RED PANDA

Published by Red Panda, an imprint of Westland Books, a division of Nasadiya Technologies Private Limited, in 2025

No. 269/2B, First Floor, 'Irai Arul', Vimalraj Street, Nethaji Nagar, Alapakkam Main Road, Maduravoyal, Chennai 600095

Westland, the Westland logo, Red Panda and the Red Panda logo are thetrademarks of Nasadiya Technologies Private Limited, or its affiliates.

ISBN: 9789360454913

10 9 8 7 6 5 4 3 2 1

Book Design by Mukul Chand

Printed at Thomson Press (India) Ltd

For little humans Paari and Meenakshi who will always be my first readers, and little elephants Thambi and Paapa who I hope find their Soul Tree some day.

CONTENTS

1

TRAGEDY STRIKES OLD MAMA'S HERD

Elephants have names. All of them do. Only humans may not understand them. But that doesn't matter—because the herd knows, and that's enough.

This is the story of an elephant calf with two names: one in elephant talk and another in Tamil. In her herd, she was known as 'Little Girl'—LG for short. And she was the unruliest of them all.

LG never listened to her mother or aunt. Not even Old Mama! The grand old lady, the matriarch of the herd, Old Mama usually ignored LG's antics, but when she got a little too unruly, she would let out a thunderous trumpet. That would keep LG in check for about a week. And then she would start all over again.

One summer, after walking for days, the herd reached a tea plantation—a place Old

Mama called the 'danger zone'. LG was in one of her boisterous moods. Mother tried to keep her close, pushing her into that cosy space between her legs, but LG had other plans. This was a new plantation and there were so many interesting nooks for her to explore.

Old Mama was talking to Mother about the past. Many decades ago, this plantation used to be a forest with gigantic trees and thick, short shrubs that brushed against their legs. Mother was all ears, especially since Old Mama was describing in detail the sweet grass that had once grown there—the kind Mother had loved when she was a calf.

But LG was in no mood for stories.

She slipped away, dodging Old Aunt and her younger sister Grouchy Grandma who guarded the rear. The moment she was free, LG dashed into a path lined with dense tea plants on either side. What an adventure! Her tiny trunk swayed from side to side as she ran and ran. Everything around looked new and

exciting. A narrow passage to her left led her down a dirt road. Beyond it stood a shed with a water pot in front.

Thirsty, LG sucked up the water with her trunk, squirting it into her mouth. She still hadn't mastered the art of drinking like an adult, using both the trunk and the mouth. So she made a mess—tipping the pot over and watching it roll down the slope. Delighted, LG chased after it.

Until everything turned dark.

LG hadn't noticed the sun setting. Her herd had moved ahead without her. The little one called out for her mother.

No answer.

Then she called for Old Mama, despite being a little scared of her. Surely the wise matriarch would come to her rescue! But she heard nothing. Saw nothing.

LG trembled. She curled up next to a large boulder. She shut her eyes tight and cried herself to sleep.

Meanwhile, Old Mama sensed something was wrong. It was too quiet. Where was LG? Old Mama stopped in her tracks and called for her granddaughter. How foolish of her to have left the little one out of her sight! Mother, lost in memories of the delicious leaves from her childhood, still hadn't noticed that her baby was missing.

Before they could search for her, a loud blast shattered the silence. Fireworks.

Old Mama had led them right into a human settlement. Not her fault—it was not supposed to be there in the first place. Bright lights flashed. Explosions followed. People were lighting firecrackers to chase away the elephants. The animals ran amok in confusion, despite Old Mama hollering at them to stay together.

She tried to gather them but fear had taken hold. Calves stumbled. Adults trumpeted in alarm. Grouchy Grandma's grandson slipped on a glass bottle and skidded towards a steep incline.

Old Mama lunged forward.

With one swift move, she pushed the calf to safety—but she couldn't stop herself. She had run too fast and couldn't control her speed. Old Mama tumbled into the valley, trumpeting loudly. She was not scared of dying. She was scared for the herd she was supposed to protect, for her granddaughter in whom she saw herself.

Two days later, the herd reunited in the forest beyond the plantation. But something was wrong. Old Mama was missing! Mother, already in agony over losing her little girl, hid amidst the tall grass. She barely ate in her grief. Grouchy Grandma approached her, gently placing her trunk on hers.

Grouchy rumbled softly, speaking to Mother in deep, low notes. She was too old to lead. Someone else had to take charge.

The herd waited.

Grouchy spoke to Mother for a long time. Dusk had set in and fireflies came out to play.

Finally, Mother walked out from the curtain of grass and rumbled back at Grouchy Grandma.

She strode to the front of the herd and started walking. First, they had to find water; she knew most of them were thirsty. The herd followed her silently. Grandma kept the rear as usual, and Old Aunt came up to walk next to Mother. The calves hopped and skipped, occupying that safe space between Mother and Old Aunt's legs.

But Mother's eyes searched the shadows.

Where was her baby girl?

2

THE LOST ELEPHANT

L G had never felt more scared in her life. 'Old Mama?' she called—then, 'Mother? Mother!' Her voice trembled. Two men peered at her, speaking to each other in a strange language. LG understood nothing! But that didn't stop her from demanding to be taken back to her mother at once. 'Where's my mother?' she squealed.

A little later, one of the men offered her water from a wide-mouthed container. She drank to her heart's content, realising only then how thirsty she had been. He then held her trunk—his hand was softer than she'd expected—and led her into a pick-up truck.

For three days, they drove through the forest searching for the herd, unaware that it had moved deep into the jungle. On the third day, the man who kept offering her water and milk through a tube looked at her and said, 'We're sorry, little girl. You're going to have to join the camp.'

LG blinked, extended her trunk and seemed to say to him, 'I'm hungry.'

Much like her, he couldn't understand her—she didn't know his words, and he didn't know hers. The elephant camp lay on the periphery of the forest. It was home to thirty-five elephants: twenty males and fifteen females, all either abandoned as calves or captured after repeatedly straying into human habitation. They did small tasks such as carrying grass for fodder or sometimes helping the men rescue and capture other wild elephants. But, mostly, they were free to graze in the surrounding forests all day. Their caretaker, the mahout, accompanied them. They took long baths at the river in the mornings and relished mammoth balls of rice, millets and jaggery, and even whole coconuts in the evenings.

LG peered out from the back of the truck as it came to a stop. She was relieved. The constant movement had made her dizzy. She was happy to be still at last.

She stepped gingerly on an inclined wooden plank and walked down. Once on solid ground, she took a deep breath and shook her trunk this way and that, as was her habit. She stretched it to feel her mother's feet ... wait ... where was she?

Her chest tightened. 'Mother?' she cried. 'Are you there? I'm hungry.' She trotted a little, but the two men who had found her rushed forward to hold her back.

'Let me go! If Old Mama finds out that you took me away from my herd, she'll hurl you over the mountain with her trunk! Move back!'

A few more men ran up to her, some jumping off vehicles similar to the one she had ridden in. They spoke urgently in the same language she had heard before. LG sniffed the air. For the first time since her arrival, she caught a familiar scent: elephants! She looked around and saw two of them walk towards them at a leisurely pace from a distant clearing. But wait—a man was seated on one of them. That was strange. Still, she hopped forward, hollering, 'Grandma! Do you know where my mother is?'

The men came at her again, this time pulling her back with force. They led her into an enclosure nearby. LG didn't resist. She felt weak. No one understood her. Nothing made sense. She lay on a jute sack, tucking her trunk under her folded feet.

Then, the food arrived! A man—she was beginning to like him—gently touched her back and spoke in a soft, musical tone. He offered her milk from a tube connected to a plastic bottle. LG drank eagerly. She was starving. She drank so much that she forgot to breathe. She paused, swayed and almost toppled over. The man caught her. He was smiling at her. LG smiled back.

'Isn't there a way to find my baby?' Mother asked Grouchy Grandma.

'No, woman,' she replied, bluntly. They didn't call her grouchy for nothing.

Mother sighed loudly, scaring a red-wattled lapwing by her feet. The bird had been searching for a place to lay eggs and was quite annoyed with the elephant herd that had plonked itself onto her home ground.

'Besides, we are quite far from the forests where...,' Grouchy paused, '...where Old Mama died.' After a moment of consideration, she added, 'LG is probably somewhere in that neighbourhood.'

'Shall we go back?' Mother asked.

'And risk losing more elephants? Be responsible. You're not just a mother now. You are a matriarch. Think like one. Place the herd before your personal interests. That's what Old Mama would have done.'

Mother grunted. She was not liking this matriarch business one bit. All she wanted to do was run away—far, far away to where her baby girl was. To rescue her. To nourish her with milk. To hold her close. She wondered what LG was eating.

'That's enough rest, don't you think?' Grouchy rumbled. 'We better get moving.'

Mother rolled her eyes. 'Very well.'

3
LIFE AT
THE ELEPHANT CAMP

L G spent the whole of her first day at the camp clinging to a low plastic stool in a corner. She did sip milk—on and off. On her second day, she took a few small steps about, her trunk touching and feeling objects around her: a bucket, a piece of cloth, a length of rope. On the third day, she was ready to explore. She stood up and grabbed the first thing within her reach: a plastic mug. 'Hmm,' she rumbled, lifting it. Then, she dropped it, and it cracked. Her mahout, Maaran, came running inside, alarmed. When he saw her, he chuckled. He then led her outside to a fenced-in area nearby—her very own playpen!

LG walked, trotted, ran—what fun! Her trunk shook in the wind, and for a moment, she forgot all about her family. Suddenly, she heard something. Elephants. LG stopped to stare.

Camp elephants and their mahouts marched in, one behind the other, returning from their day of grazing. There were tuskers, calves much older than LG and grand old ladies, each arranging themselves in front of a low wooden fence facing the feeding room. LG watched as the mahouts left their side to bring them large balls of food, which the elephants eagerly caught in their mouths. She wondered if she, too, would get some.

As they began to disperse, an older female walked past LG. 'You poor little thing,' she tut-tutted. 'We've been talking about you all day,' she said, pausing. Their mahouts were chatting too.

'Do you know where my mother is, Grandma?' LG asked.

The older elephant shook her head.

'Old Mama must be looking for me,' LG added firmly.

'Did you say Old Mama?'

'Yes, I did,' replied LG.

'My goodness me! We used to be friends!' squealed the old elephant. 'You say you're her granddaughter? Look at you! You look just like her.'

LG grinned.

The elephant introduced herself: 'I'm Flappy Ears by the way. I'm seventy years old.'

'And I'm Little Girl!' exclaimed LG. 'I'm eleven months old. They call me LG for short.'

'Tell me, Flappy Grandma, how do I get out of here? I want to see my mother. I miss her dearly.'

Flappy fell silent. 'I will tell you tomorrow. Same time. Can you wait just a day?'

'Of course!' replied LG. 'I can wait a day.'

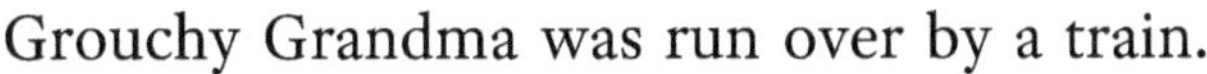

Grouchy Grandma was run over by a train.

Mother had unwittingly led them down a new path, as over a dozen brick kilns had sprung up on their usual migratory route. She didn't recall seeing train tracks the last time she passed through with her herd. They had all crossed to safety, reaching the forest on the other side when a train came thundering down the track. Grouchy, who was getting slower due to age, slipped on the sharp rocks strewn around the track and fell. By the time she got back on her feet, it was all over. The train struck her at full speed.

The herd was devastated. Their youngest was missing, and now two of their elders were dead. Mother did her best to keep their morale high, but she knew she was faltering. *Dear God, help my herd,* she prayed, placing her trunk on a mammoth tree. This was no ordinary tree. For Mother's clan, this was the god they worshipped.

Elephants divided themselves into herds that worshiped trees, soil, water and the sky. Each herd had its own preferences, passed down through generations, forming clans with distinct beliefs. Despite their differences, an unspoken rule among clans was that they were all equal.

Old Mama had taught her herd that their god resided in trees and plants, best reached through touch. 'Nothing like a good trunk-to-trunk,' she would joke, urging them to spend at least a few minutes a day praying to the trees of the forest.

One by one, the other elephants in the herd started to imitate Mother. They arranged themselves in a circle around the tree, placing their trunks on its trunk. They all thought of Old Mama and Grouchy Grandma at that moment and prayed for the safety of their young and their elders. Eyes closed, they rumbled in unison, their ears and tails unmoving.

'If you're listening, mother of trees,' Mother whispered. 'Please help my daughter, wherever she is. Protect her. Give her back to me. Please, I ask nothing else of you.'

Meanwhile, LG waited patiently for Flappy Ears to pass by the next evening. But when she did, she simply waved and called out, 'Tomorrow, LG. I'm in a hurry.' She did the same for a full week.

On the eighth day, LG lost her patience. She jumped at Flappy, trying to punch her wrinkled feet. 'Stop! You liar!' she screamed. 'You were making a fool out of me,' LG wailed.

Flappy Ears looked at her with tears in her eyes. She did not have the heart to tell her that she would spend the rest of her life at the camp as a tamed elephant.

'I'm sorry,' Flappy whispered. 'I lied.' She did feel guilty about doing so but was not brave enough to tell her the truth.

LG was sure there was a way out. There just had to be! She was comfortable, yes. Her mahout took good care of her, fed her milk whenever she was hungry and even learned to recognise her hunger cues. He slept outside her enclosure, took her for strolls in her playpen and was at her beck and call all day and night. But he was not her mother.

That night, LG stepped out of her enclosure and sprawled out on the short grass in the front. The air was cold. Stars filled the sky but the moon was nowhere in sight. She wondered if she could just take off into the forest on her own. But the men had things with wheels. They would bring her back in no time.

Then, she noticed a massive tree a short distance away. It had heart-shaped leaves, and its trunk was as wide as a full-grown elephant. Its roots spread out like a web beneath it, and LG felt drawn to it for some reason.

She found a cosy spot among the roots and snuggled inside, falling asleep with her head resting against the trunk.

Flappy Ears stood in the river as her mahout scrubbed her back with coconut fibre. This was their morning ritual—her favourite part of the day. She stood still, eyes half-closed, enjoying the attention.

'Have you any guilt?'

Startled, Flappy opened her eyes. It was her friend and fellow camp elephant, Two Trunks. She was named so for her exceptionally long trunk. She was as old as Flappy. Unlike some of the temperamental seniors who rudely trumpeted at the younger ones when their mahouts weren't looking, Two Trunks was kind to everyone.

'What do you mean?' Flappy asked her, looking confused.

'I'm talking about that poor baby girl. The new one. You gave her false hope. That was wrong,' said Two Trunks, gently lifting one of her front legs to let her mahout mount and scrub her head.

'News spreads fast at the camp, I see,' muttered Flappy.

Two Trunks snorted. 'There's nothing much to do around here, is there?'

'I was just trying to cheer her up,' Flappy said defensively.

'Nonsense! You just enjoyed the attention,' Two Trunks snapped.

'How dare you say such a thing!' Flappy was fuming. Her mahout looked at her, worried. She did her best to hide her anger from him. Years of training had taught her to hide her true feelings from everyone around her, especially humans. 'I was just trying to make conversation. She looked up at me with so much hope ... I was at a loss,' Flappy explained, her head bent low. Her mahout slapped her trunk, signalling her to look up.

Two Trunks remained unfazed. 'If you truly want to help her, why not make it up to her?' Then, she added, in a hushed trumpet, 'I mean, it's not like the two of us are doing anything productive around here. Let's just help this calf find her herd before we die of bitterness and old age, shall we?'

Flappy looked at her friend, bewildered. 'Are you nuts? Has any elephant ever left this camp once it was brought here? You're turning senile, Two,' she scoffed.

'Listen, Flappy. Have you heard of the legend of the Soul Tree?' Two Trunks asked, her voice now a whisper.

Flappy frowned. 'Soul Tree? Is this another one of those silly campfire tales? Like that Youth Fall that's supposed to make you younger?'

'For once, stop being sarcastic,' Two Trunks shot her down. 'The Soul Tree is a sacred gateway into distant lands,' she explained. 'You must've heard of it as a child. It is a gift reserved for elephants from the tree clan. I know of many camp elephants who spent all their youth looking for it. But no one has ever found it ... they are all here as you can see....'

Their mahouts finished bathing them and led them out to graze. Two Trunks continued, as the two elephants pulled up clumps of grass. 'I heard Killer knows where it is,' she whispered.

Flappy froze, a bamboo shoot snapping in her trunk. 'Wait … you mean *that* Killer?' she replied, breathing hard. She dropped the shoot and looked her friend straight in the eye: 'I'm *not* talking to that fellow. He killed seven people and is now in musth! There's a reason he's been tied to a tree far away from the camp. Musth is when young males are in peak form and energy—raring to go. You know that, right?'

'Let's try, shall we? Please Flappy, I'm sure he's not as terrible as they make him out to be,' said Two Trunks, looking at her friend expectantly.

Flappy sighed. 'Alright. Let's go around lunchtime when our mahouts take a nap. Spray some of that "sunsleep" flower nectar on the two of them, will you? There are plenty of those flowers behind that big boulder by the river. The men will be out cold for a long time, and we can get our job done without being seen.'

Two Trunks nodded. Camp elephants had long known this trick for sneaking beyond the grazing boundaries. Humans had no idea!

Once their mahouts were asleep, the two elephants slowly walked up a hillock.

'You know,' said Two Trunks, 'I once tried to run away after spraying a good amount of sunsleep nectar on my mahout.' The ascent was harder than Flappy remembered. She was getting old, she thought bitterly; her feet ached.

Flappy groaned. 'Yes, I've heard this story *many* times.'

But Two Trunks went on, as though she never heard her friend. 'I crossed the boundary in no time—I'd eaten double my portion of grass that morning. I was ready to walk far. I only managed to cross a few dozen trees from the camp when I started feeling jittery.

I wasn't exactly a wild elephant anymore, you know.... I needed to be accepted into a herd to survive....'

The elephants took a short break to eat some freshly sprouted grass at the top of the hillock. Flappy noticed with delight that they were covered in dew, making them soft and juicy. Two Trunks grabbed a trunkful, before continuing her story.

'That was fifty years ago ... but I remember everything as though it happened yesterday. So, back then, there was a tiger on the prowl, very close to the camp. I had heard from the other elephants that it was quite the rogue and wouldn't hesitate to bring down a full-grown elephant. He was called Fire, remember? They said his coat would shine, as though it were ablaze.'

'Yes, yes,' Flappy said distractedly. She was busy relishing the grass.

'Well, there was a small clearing, and I had decided to rest my feet there for a while. Then,

I heard it—a growl from the bushes a distance away. The leaves trembled, and I swear I saw a flash of orange. It was Fire, alright! I knew if he realised I was a camp elephant, he'd hunt me down! I stood up, trembling from head to foot. Fire growled once again and I ran for my life! I was back at the camp in no time. My mahout was still asleep. I never ever tried leaving again!'

'But you don't even know if it *was* Fire,' Flappy Ears said, her voice muffled from all the chewing.

'I'm not stupid,' Two Trunks snapped.

Flappy Ears said nothing.

'There he is. Shall we?' asked her friend.

They had arrived.

The two elephants gulped. They were not fearless—not here anyway. Approaching Killer—especially while he was musth—was madness. Many bull elephants had even killed their mahouts in such a state.

Yet, they stepped forward.

4

MEETING WITH THE MIGHTY KILLER

Killer was one of the newest members of the elephant camp. He was a thirty-eight-year-old tusker. A hill on the fringes of his home range held an ancient temple where regular visitors would offer him coconuts and bananas whenever he ventured outside. Emboldened, he started entering the nearby village. The first person he killed—a young man who had come out to relieve himself at night—threw a sickle at the elephant to defend himself. Killer had approached him, expecting food. Caught off guard by the man's reaction, Killer swung his trunk at him in defence, killing him instantly.

Over the years, people in the village and nearby settlements grew to fear Killer. But the elephant believed they were harmless. He never understood human behaviour.

While some pampered him with food, others hurled stones at him and chased him back into the forest. Heartbroken and confused, he had hurt many people, killing several in the process. No one realised that deep down he was just a wounded elephant—fooled into trusting humans.

When Killer saw the two females approach him, he instantly became alert. Something was wrong. None of the camp elephants ever came near him when he was in musth isolation. He had been tied to a tree for several weeks ever since his mahout discovered he was in his yearly musth. Killer hated this period when other elephants kept away from him. But he had heard from both people and elephants that he became aggressive during this time. No matter how much he tried to resist, his mahout always tied him far from the others and starved him so he would return to normal.

'Does he look thinner?' whispered Two Trunks as Killer came into view.

'Yes, don't you know? That's what they do ... they barely feed bull elephants in musth so they can calm down faster,' Flappy replied.

The two of them stood at a distance of four trunks from Killer who let out a series of low rumbles. Flappy placed her trunk on Two Trunks' shoulder. 'Should we turn back?' she whispered. 'I'm scared.'

Then, Killer laughed. He laughed so hard that the tree he was tied to shook. 'Come closer, you cowards,' he said between spurts of laughter. 'I kill humans, not elephants.' He paused, looking at the females, howling with laughter. 'Just look at how you're trembling!'

'We're here to talk,' said Two Trunks. 'There's something we need to ask you. I am Two Trunks and this is my friend, Flappy Ears.'

Killer made a small circle by his feet with his trunk, saying, 'Go on,' watching a black millipede zigzag through the dent in the earth his trunk had carved.

Flappy Ears noticed how he nudged the millipede away from the tree, where a grey hornbill sat, eager to catch the insect. The millepede eventually found a boulder nearby and disappeared behind it. The hornbill flew away.

'Do you know where the Soul Tree is?' Two Trunks asked.

Killer looked up at her. 'What did you say? Come again.'

'You heard her,' Flappy replied, peeved. She knew he had heard the question loud and clear.

'You're right, old lady,' Killer sniggered. 'Grandma's getting annoyed, I see.'

Flappy Ears lifted her trunk and trumpeted a warning. 'Respect, young man. Didn't your mother teach you to respect your elders?'

Two Trunks looked at her friend with pride—talking back at Killer!

'Sorry, Grandma,' Killer drawled, standing up. 'I've been lonely, you see. Forgot my manners.' He chuckled, pulling bark off the tree and biting into the sap-filled inner portion.

Flappy Ears noticed that he had stripped almost the entire tree.

'First, I need some information. Tell me—how are my dear brothers, Tall Boy and Brown Tusk? Are they missing me? And my sisters ... I sure miss their questions about the outside world. I heard a mahout broke his leg. Is there a new calf at the camp now? And oh, I also got word of a tourist throwing a bunch of bananas at Old Grey's face. Is he alright?'

The two female elephants blinked. How did he know so much, despite being away from the camp for over a month?

Killer, reading their expressions, smirked. 'I've got sources everywhere, ladies.' He extended his trunk to the right for a jungle babbler to perch on. 'This bird here is one of my friends. I can't understand her, but she never stops chattering. Listening to her keeps me sane. Her whole family moves together, tree to tree.'

Flappy Ears looked at the goofy tusker who clearly enjoyed camp gossip and showing off. Who on earth named him Killer? Clown would've been a better name!

'Your silliness does not suit that very daring name,' she chuckled. 'Ever considered changing your name to Clown?'

Killer's expression darkened. He rumbled and mock-charged at them, sending red dust flying all around. This time, he was not joking. 'Is that better?' he thundered.

'You fool,' screamed Two Trunks. 'Look what you've done! You've angered the Killer himself.'

When the dust settled, the two females saw Killer standing very still—now three more pairs of jungle babblers perched on his tusks, chirping non-stop. It was an amusing sight—hardly what one would expect from an aggressive elephant. How quickly he had composed himself!

'Sorry about that, Flappy. I sure should learn to take a joke,' he said.

Flappy Ears was beginning to like him.

'All the elephants you asked after are doing well,' Two Trunks recounted. 'Yes, a mahout broke his leg when he slipped on a rock near the river. He's not shown up in a week. The tourist who misbehaved was sent away. Luckily for him, Old Grey was in a good mood, and yes, about the new member. She's a baby, still on her mother's milk. We need your help to reunite her with her herd.'

'Me? My help?' Killer chuckled, startling the babblers into flight. 'How am I supposed to do that? They won't even let me enter the camp for another three weeks! You grandmas are turning—'

'Tell us about the Soul Tree,' said Two Trunks flatly.

Killer froze mid-sentence. 'How do you know about the Soul Tree?'

'Come on, Killer,' Two Trunks said. 'Stop acting as though you know nothing. Every elephant, irrespective of their clan, knows about the Soul Tree. But not many know where it is.'

'What makes you think I do?' Killer shot back.

'You are from the west, aren't you? All elephants from the west are tree worshippers. We know that. Your matriarch must've told you. It's part of a herd's code of conduct,' Two Trunks ventured.

Killer looked genuinely surprised. Three decades ago when he was still under his mother's care, she had once whispered to him, 'You will leave the herd in a few years, son. If ever you get lost and when you have absolutely nowhere to go, seek the Soul Tree.' She then explained how to find it.

Killer, however, had never gone looking for it—not once in all these years. He was happy wherever he was—until now.

'There is one problem,' he finally said. 'This knowledge is passed on from the matriarch to the younger ones. I do not have the right to do so.'

'We break rules all the time!' Flappy Ears scoffed.

Killer took a deep breath. 'You say she is from the tree clan?'

'Yes,' replied Flappy, hopeful. 'I knew her grandmother.'

'Then I guess I could tell her where the tree is. Only tree clan elephants should know, so I don't think we will be breaking any rules.'

Two Trunks almost jumped with joy. She grasped Flappy's trunk, and the two old elephants smiled at each other, relieved.

Killer smirked. 'But I won't do it for free.'

'You greedy tusker—' Two Trunks began.

'I need salt to eat. I've been craving it for a long time. I don't care much for food. But I can't live without salt. They store salt in those small packets in the feeding room at camp. We can't enter. But the calf should be small enough to walk through the door. Ask her to sneak in and bring me a packet tonight. I will then reveal the secret about the Soul Tree.'

'You—' Flappy began.

'Enough! I'm sleepy, ladies. Now if you two can make way for some air around here....'

'But...' said Flappy Ears.

'I cannot share the information with elephants from other clans. I don't know which one you two are from but I'm sure it's not Tree. Please leave now. Tell the girl not to be too late. I go to sleep when the moon touches the mountain tips.'

Saying so, Killer turned away, settling down to take a nap.

The two elephants looked at each other, shook their heads and slowly made their way back to the camp in silence.

5

AN ACT OF STEALTH ON A STARRY NIGHT

LG lay on her side outside her enclosure, resting her head on a cool patch of damp earth. It had rained the previous night. She thought of her mother constantly. She missed nuzzling against her soft, warm underbelly. Only now did LG realise how protected she had been with her herd. Mother, her aunts, Old Mama—none of them had let her out of their sight. Mother always kept her safe within her four magnificent legs. LG sighed. How she wished she had listened to the seniors in her herd.

It had been two weeks since she arrived at the camp, and she felt weak. Her mahout, who doted on her, did his best—LG saw how his face fell whenever she refused milk. But she just didn't like it. It was nothing like her mother's milk, and she wanted only that.

She saw two grandma elephants walking towards her. LG recognised Flappy Ears instantly but did not know the other elephant, though she had noticed her at the camp.

'How are you, LG?' Flappy asked, panting.

'I'm okay,' replied LG glumly.

'Oh, don't be sad. We bring you good news,' Two Trunks joined in and introduced herself.

LG stood up but her legs gave away. Her legs had no strength in them.

'But,' said Flappy Ears. 'You appear very delicate. I doubt if you can take it.'

'Wait right here,' squealed LG, tottering her way into the enclosure. She butted her head against Maaran's shoulder. He was sweeping the floor. He quickly brought her some milk to drink. LG sucked every last drop through the tube as the man watched, tears in his eyes. He had feared his elephant calf would die if she continued to starve.

LG came trotting outside, her little trunk swaying from left to right. She was ready!

Flappy Ears smiled at the sight of the adorable little elephant. She couldn't wait for LG to be back with her herd.

'Tell me, Flappy and Two Trunks. I'm ready,' she said, burping.

Two Trunks began. 'Have you heard about elephant clans, LG?'

LG shook her head. Two Trunks had expected this. Initiation into clan code of conduct and worship usually started only after calves turned eight years old.

'There are four in total: Tree, Soil, Water and Sky. Your matriarch will tell you more about each of them. What you need to know is that you are from the tree clan.'

LG listened without batting an eyelid.

'Tree elephants worship, as the name implies, trees and plants. They believe there's life in everything green. And when you place your trust in anything in this forest, little one, it will never betray you.'

LG shivered. She had goosebumps all over her little body.

Maaran stepped outside and was taken aback to see the three elephants huddled together. It appeared as though they were having a conversation. He considered fetching the mahouts of the older elephants. But then he remembered how LG had suddenly come running to drink milk after refusing to touch it for days. Something was up! Over forty years of tending to elephants had taught him one key lesson: elephants could never be fully understood.

He had often been spellbound by their behaviour but never spoke about it with the scientists and doctors who studied them at the camp. Certain things could not be explained in words.

And so, that day, Maaran decided to go back inside and wait until LG finished whatever she was doing.

Meanwhile, Flappy and Two Trunks continued with their sermon. 'Each clan is eligible for gifts from their gods,' Two Trunks said. 'These are little things that help us when we are in trouble. We can use each gift just once in our lifetime.'

'Among the tree clan's gifts, the mother of all gifts, so to speak, is the Soul Tree,' said Flappy. 'This tree can take you to any part of the forest you wish to go to.'

LG gasped. 'Where is it, Flappy?' she asked excitedly. 'Where is the Soul Tree?'

Flappy then told her about Killer, explaining that he was from LG's clan and willing to share the secret of the Soul Tree.

LG was both excited and nervous. She had never done anything on her own. Her mother, grandma and aunts were always there to take care of her needs. Now, she must set out into the forest all by herself. LG realised she had to put her fears aside if she wanted to return to her herd.

'I've never interacted much with tuskers,' she said. 'Even Old Mama keeps away from some of them. I always wondered why. I can't wait to meet him! But where is Killer?' she asked.

Flappy and Two Trunks also told her why he was named so. For some reason, he did not scare her. Her herd, too, once had a tusker who separated and became quite the ruffian. But he was always kind to smaller elephants whenever they crossed paths.

'There is something he wants in exchange for this information,' Two Trunks said, shaking her head. She told LG about Killer's demand. 'He can be quite a pain at times,' she added.

LG chuckled. 'This does seem simple. The feeding room is right here,' she said, pointing to the tin-roofed structure near the enclosure. 'I've seen men mix that white stuff—you say it's called salt?—with the rice and millet balls during feeding sessions. I'll sneak in, grab some and run to the hillock.'

Flappy Ears was impressed by LG's confidence. She had half expected the calf to be afraid of entering the feeding room alone at night. But no—she seemed rather thrilled about the whole thing.

'Are you sure you can do this?' Two Trunks asked, after briefing LG on how to get to the hillock where Killer was kept.

'Yes, Two. The man—'

'We call them mahouts,' Flappy offered.

'Oh, thanks! My ma-mahout sleeps all night. He won't notice a thing. I'll be back before he wakes up,' LG added.

The elephants stood in a huddle for a long time. Flappy Ears hesitated to let LG leave the safe confines of her enclosure. But she knew that if any of the adult elephants walked up the hillock at night, they would surely draw attention. Due to her size, LG would not be noticed easily.

'Be careful, LG,' Flappy Ears said. 'Both of us will be awake, our ears peeled for any sounds from the hillock ... in case there's any mishap.'

'Oh, come on, Flappy,' Two Trunks started walking away. 'This is nothing. Don't scare her. Besides, her real adventure is yet to begin.' She dragged Flappy Ears away, who kept turning back to wave at LG.

LG stood there until both the elephants were out of sight, then went back inside. She was hungry once again.

It was the night before the full moon, and the stars shone against a cloudless sky. LG waited for her mahout to go to sleep. She had drunk her milk and was ready. The feeding room was very close to her enclosure, and she had no qualms about entering it. She was confident about finding the salt. But the walk uphill to Killer made her anxious. She would be all alone, and she was scared of tigers and dholes. Flappy Ears had warned her about two packs of dholes in the vicinity. What if they decided to come out?

She stepped outside, and the air felt cold against her skin. *I'll deal with the dholes if and when I see them*, she told herself. Her feet trembled as she swiftly crossed the space between her enclosure and the feeding room's back wall. She kept turning back to see if anyone was following her. No. There was no one outside but the insects of the night.

She pushed open the wooden door of the room and spotted the salt immediately. It was placed on a long, raised platform that functioned as a table on which food for the camp elephants was arranged in a row during feeding time. She grabbed the packet, spilling some on the platform.

She thought she heard something that sounded like an animal growling. LG stood very still. No—it was only the wind. She held the packet tightly with her trunk and went out, looking at the hillock up ahead. LG

drew a deep breath and trotted towards her destination.

Luckily for her, the path was well-lit by the moon and the stars. She was halfway there when she paused to catch her breath. She looked up and saw Killer. He stood erect, looking at her. LG could not see his features clearly. He was silhouetted against the moon, his massive tusks thrusting out magnificently. LG thought he was awe-inspiring. She gripped the packet of salt and plodded on, reaching the tree to which Killer was tied in just under twenty minutes.

'Hi,' said LG, looking Killer in the eye.

'Do you have what I asked for?' he snarled.

'Ye-yes,' replied LG, startled by his tone. She wasn't expecting this.

'Come closer,' he ordered, adding, 'Hand it to me.'

LG took a few short steps forward, hesitantly. She held out the packet for him. It was empty! LG shook it in disbelief. She had spilled all the salt along the way. She looked down at her feet, dismayed.

'Well?' asked Killer. 'There is nothing in there.'

'I'm sorry…,' LG said softly. She was on the verge of tears. All her effort was wasted. How foolish she had been. 'I spilled it all!'

'All of it?'

'All of it.'

Killer laughed. It took a few moments for LG to realise that he was actually laughing at the situation. She relaxed.

'Come here,' Killer called to her, and LG went up to him. He touched her head with his trunk ever so gently and said, 'That was very brave of you, fellow clan elephant.'

'I'm LG,' she told him.

'Oh yes, LG,' Killer went on. 'I don't care about the salt. You tried and that's enough. Thank you.'

6

THE SACRED GATEWAY

L G waited for Killer to talk about the Soul Tree. She was exhausted and wanted to return to her enclosure and sleep before her mahout woke up.

'Come here, sit down next to me,' Killer said, settling down to face the camp.

LG followed suit.

'You're too young to be spending your life in an elephant camp,' Killer began, glancing at her sideways. 'You have everything here— great food, great company and mahouts who love you like their own children. But there's one thing that you will not have, till your last breath: freedom.'

He paused to look at the moon before continuing. 'Freedom to roam the forests day and night. Freedom to live with a herd that will die to protect you. Freedom to live on your terms. I know I will never have any of that. And every single day, I ask myself: why do I live like a domestic animal when in fact I was made for the wild?'

'Then why don't you leave, Killer?' LG asked. 'You know where the Soul Tree is....'

'That's a good question,' Killer said. 'But I cannot go back to where I came from. I placed my trust in the wrong kind of living beings. And camp life ... it does something to you. I don't know how to explain it. I only know that I'm not my true self anymore. I have this fear inside me—fear of not fitting in with other wild elephants, of not surviving on my own. That is why most elephants choose to stay back, like I did. After I was caught, they pushed me into a huge vehicle. I was terrified. I didn't move an inch. Then they brought another machine, a mammoth one with a metal arm, twice as big as me. It shoved me into the vehicle. I had no choice but to clamber inside. I was trembling throughout

the journey. I still have nightmares about it. I can try to escape but what if I get caught? I cannot face that machine again—ever.'

LG hung on to his every word.

'But it's not too late for you,' Killer told her. 'If you make it to the Soul Tree, you have a shot at a better life—the life you were born into.'

He then turned to her. 'Do you know how many elephant clans there are in the world?'

'Four,' LG answered. 'Tree, Soil, Water and Sky.'

'Very good. A clan consists of fifteen to twenty herds. To use the Soul Tree, you need to know where your herd is. Even an approximate location would do. Do you have any idea where your herd might be?'

'I hope they haven't crossed the mountains yet,' said LG.

'They might not be very far since it's been only two weeks since you got separated. But you need to think carefully about where you want to go before you set out on this journey,' Killer said. Then he added, 'Now for the important part. A lifeforce enters a tree to turn it into the Soul Tree—a living, breathing being. It can be any tree, but it must grow in the soil beneath which a dead tree clan elephant is buried. You don't find the Soul Tree—it finds you. The moment you head into the forest looking for it, it will know. All the trees in the forest are connected. They send signals to each other. And when the time is right, the Soul Tree will reveal itself.'

'But how will I identify it?' LG asked.

'You just will,' Killer replied. 'It works like a door. Fix your destination in your mind, touch the tree with the tip of your trunk and it will open, taking you inside. Seconds later, you will walk out—right where you wished to be.'

'What if I end up in the wrong place?' LG asked, suddenly anxious.

'It's not like you'll land in your herd's lap,' Killer said. 'They will be somewhere close by, and you will have to search for them. But that will happen if you fix the right location in your mind.'

'So, if I choose the wrong place,' LG gulped, 'I might get lost again?'

Killer hesitated before answering. 'That is a possibility, yes.'

LG had so many questions. 'Where do I start?' she said, looking at Killer hopefully.

'You must first cross the river in the east,' Killer said, 'then walk up the blue mountains, past the teak trees, until you enter the dense shola forests. I know of several tree clan elephants buried in those forests. The vegetation there is so thick that sunlight can't make it past the tree tops on to the forest floor. Those sholas are sacred. At dawn, the sholas glow golden green from the slivers of light that manage to break through the canopy. If you're lucky, you'll find the Soul Tree within a few dozen steps. It is always an ancient tree—as ancient as our matriarchs.'

'What is the connection between dead tree-clan elephants and the Soul Tree?' LG asked. 'Why does it only appear where they are buried?'

Killer smiled. From the moment he had seen her trundle up the hillock with the empty salt packet, he had liked her. She was a fearless little elephant. And now, her questions proved she was a thinking one too.

'You're quite the bright one,' he chuckled. 'Elephants always look after their herd—even after death. Their spirits come together to form the beating heart of the Soul Tree.'

LG was stunned. She had never imagined her ancestors were capable of such magic.

'I know of several elephants who went looking for it,' Killer went on. 'But not all were successful.' Then, with a chuckle, he added, 'My theory is that only an enlightened elephant can find it. Don't ask me what enlightenment is though. I'm not enlightened enough to elaborate on the matter.'

They sat in silence for a while. Then, from a nearby patch of trees, a spotted deer with a grand pair of antlers appeared, carrying a bunch of wild berries in her mouth. She placed them under the tree and looked back. Moments later, two smaller deer emerged, carrying more of the same berries. Killer nodded at them, lifting his trunk and the three deer disappeared into the trees. It all happened so fast that LG had barely time to blink.

'Shall we eat? I'm starving,' Killer said. 'Help yourself to some deerberries. They're sour and juicy, and just a handful will fill your tummy. They are available only at night though. There's no sign of them in the mornings. The deer love them. It's their favourite, which explains why they are named after the gentle creatures.'

LG tried the golden-yellow berries. They were delicious.

'My mahout thinks starving me will tone down my aggression,' Killer laughed. 'But I have too many friends in the woods!'

With her tummy full, LG felt sleepy. Killer was talking about a leopard he was friends with when she dozed off, her head resting against his feet.

Killer noticed this and smiled. Soon, he was asleep too.

A loud buzzing near his ears jolted Killer awake. Startled, he looked around. It was a bee. He tried swatting at it with his trunk—then remembered. LG!

He nudged her awake. It was almost dawn.

LG sat up with a start. 'I have to go!'

'LG,' Killer said in a rush. 'Tonight is a full-moon night. The perfect time to go looking for the Soul Tree. The forest will be well-lit, and the stars will be on your side.'

LG nodded. 'Thank you, Killer. For everything.'

He placed his trunk gently on her head. 'You're a special little elephant. I know you'll find the Soul Tree. Run along before your mahout wakes up!'

LG took one last look at Killer, waved her trunk and ran downhill towards the camp.

7

GOODBYE, ELEPHANT CAMP

Mother knew that if they crossed the shola forests of the blue mountains and entered the scrub jungle on the plains, they would not return for another year. By then, any hope of finding her daughter would be lost. Yet, she never said a word of it to the herd.

She knew they would refuse to go back near the plantation, and neither did she have the courage to try to persuade them. Something just felt wrong. The elephants trudged with their heads hung low, barely eating. They mirrored their matriarch's mood, and Mother struggled to cheer them up—not when she was herself weighed down by grief.

As they moved, she noticed the trees thinning. Soon, they would reach the grasslands. Beyond that lay another patch of sholas, and then the journey downhill—leaving behind the mountains and her daughter forever.

She stopped before a towering bishopwood tree, its topmost tips were engulfed in clouds. She touched it with her trunk. The bark was warm. A shiver ran through her. Was this a sign from her clan god?

Without thinking, she turned to the herd. 'We halt here for three days.'

The elephants were taken aback.

'I thought we were leaving the sholas,' Lean Legs protested. 'There are young ones with us. It's not safe here. There may be tigers and hyenas too.'

'Then we will be extra cautious,' Mother replied firmly.

'But—' Lean Legs started again.

'Enough!' Mother's voice rang through the air. 'We are all tired. We need to eat well before the journey downhill. For once, Lean Legs, listen to your matriarch.'

'She is our matriarch now?' Someone sniggered from the back.

Mother could not identify the voice, but she let it go. She thought of Old Mama, and how she commanded respect effortlessly. The elephants always did exactly what she said. *It is not easy being a leader*, she thought with a sigh. *Old Mama had set high standards.*

'You are free to leave,' Mother declared. 'If you do not like your matriarch, you can leave and find another herd.'

There was silence.

The herd then settled down. A few females left in search of water. Mother sat under the bishopwood tree, watching over the calves whose mothers had gone to graze. She gazed up at the branches and whispered, 'LG, where are you?'

It was LG's last day at the elephant camp. She planned to leave after sunset, just as Killer had suggested. Restless with excitement, she pranced about in her playpen, waiting for Flappy Ears and Two Trunks. When she spotted them approaching, she let out a trumpet, hop-skipping towards them.

'He told me all about the Soul Tree! Flappy, Two Trunks, I leave tonight!'

'Calm down,' Flappy Ears laughed. 'Your mahout will get suspicious.'

The senior elephants listened as LG recounted her conversation with Killer.

'Eat well today,' Two Trunks advised. 'You're going to need lots of energy.'

Flappy was worried about LG crossing the river. She didn't want to stop the calf from trying, but it was a dangerous journey. If LG got lost again, the camp officials would launch another search operation for her. At worst, she would be captured and brought back again. There was another risk too— falling prey to hyenas or dholes if she grew too weak.

Still, Flappy Ears believed in LG. The little calf had changed so much since her arrival at the camp. She was no longer the meek little calf who broke into tears ten times a day. She was LG, granddaughter of the mighty Old Mama—ready to take on the sholas all by herself.

Flappy Ears felt proud of the little one. She patted LG on the head and said, 'Come visit us when you're all grown up. I'm sure you will lead your own herd one day.'

LG was touched by the concern. She didn't know what to say.

'Be careful out there. Stay safe,' Two Trunks murmured.

Maaran was watching them from a distance. He had a feeling his elephant was planning to run. He had seen her sneak into the enclosure early that morning and wondered where she had been all night. Elephants attempted to escape often, but Maaran had never heard of a calf trying the same.

8

PREDATORS ON THE PROWL

The forest was bathed in a silvery glow. The full moon shone bright, like a golden ball dipped in cream-white paint. LG glanced at her mahout—he was fast asleep. Slipping out of her playpen silently, she rushed to the fringes of the forest.

Her heart was pounding. At that moment, she wanted to go back into the safe confines of the enclosure—her home for the past two weeks. But she shuddered at the thought. She was beginning to think like a tamed elephant. LG remembered what Killer had told her.

She hurried into familiar territory. The forest was not new to her. The moonlit path stretched ahead, and she strode forward, her trunk extended in front. After walking for a while, she paused to listen to the sound of water. The river was close by. She could smell it already.

She continued forward. Strange. The earth beneath her feet felt soft. LG hesitated. Then came a loud squelch. She looked down—her feet were sinking into mud! She took one more step and suddenly found herself falling.

LG cried out! She had walked right into the riverbank! She tumbled below rapidly, stopping inches from the water. Her trunk had instinctively grabbed onto a protruding root, halting her fall. Below her, the river flowed gently, as though nothing had happened.

LG had to act fast. Her grip on the root was slipping. If she fell into the river—even though the current wasn't strong—she would surely be swept away. She had never crossed a river in her life.

Then, something unexpected happened.

Loose earth crumbled onto her head. She looked up. Wait! Was that a human voice? The sound of the surging river filled her ears, and she had not heard her name being called out. It was her mahout!

Maaran carefully slid down the riverbank, stopping next to LG. He reached out, and LG instinctively offered him her trunk. He placed another hand around her shoulder, gently guiding her downward till they stood firmly on the river's edge.

The water barely covered her toes.

The river, which originated in the mountains, flowed through acres and acres of forest land before reaching this point. The section LG was meant to cross was narrow, and luckily, since it was summer, the water was shallow.

She wondered if it was all over. Would her mahout take her back to camp?

'Are you going home?' he seemed to ask her. LG looked at him, puzzled. Then, to her utter disbelief, he led her into the river, still holding her trunk.

'I will help you cross, then you are on your own,' he added. Maaran, whose father and grandfather were mahouts too, had heard stories about elephants coming back for their

calves if they got separated. He hoped LG's mother was somewhere beyond the river.

LG realised he was helping her, not stopping her. She followed him, carefully planting her feet on the riverbed, which was filled with pebbles. She almost slipped a few times and was grateful that Maaran was there to help her.

The water rose to her shoulder as they reached the middle of the river. Slowly, they made their way across. As they reached the other bank, LG grew jubilant. She had done it! She went around in circles, doing her usual happy dance—her little trunk flapping up and down.

Maaran smiled at her. She then stopped and walked closer to him. He knelt, placing his forehead against hers, breathing in deeply. They remained in the embrace for a while, as the water gurgled on.

'I knew you were special, Paapa,' he whispered and kissed her prickly forehead covered in brown baby hair.

Paapa.

She'd heard that word before.

LG recalled Maaran addressing her as Paapa all the time. She now understood: he had named her Paapa. Not bad, she thought. LG Paapa. She liked the sound of it.

'Go,' Maaran said, giving LG a gentle push. She clambered up the bank. This one was not steep thankfully. She turned to look at Maaran one last time, before disappearing into the forest.

LG walked for over an hour before stopping to rest. Her feet hurt, but she was not thirsty. She had drunk plenty at the river. She sat under a tree. She couldn't tell what kind it was in the dark. Her eyelids grew heavy.

'Keep moving, LG. There is no time to rest,' Old Mama's voice rumbled.

LG's ears twitched. She could hear her grandmother loud and clear but could not see her. It were as though the sound came from the sky. Or, perhaps from the ground? Or the trees around her?

'The forest is not a safe place for an elephant calf alone.'

Before LG could react, the ground beneath her gave way. She plunged into a dark nothingness—falling right into the arms of a root. It was thick and gnarled, and LG was sure it was hundreds of years old.

Old Mama's voice floated by once again, and this time, it was louder. In fact, it was so loud that LG's ears hurt.

'Old Mama, stop!' she exclaimed, opening her eyes.

LG was right under the tree where she had dozed off.

Was it a dream?

It had felt all too real.

Whatever it was, LG decided to do as Old Mama had said—keep walking.

She started again, her head a little fuzzy from the dream. She wondered why she only heard Old Mama and did not see her. Was her grandma alright?

A little distance on, LG heard an animal whimpering.

She looked around and spotted a small dhole pup emerging from a bush. Its coat was the colour of rust.

'Aww, look at you!' LG cooed. 'Come here, little one. Are you lost, like me?'

The pup whimpered louder.

'Shhh, don't do that,' LG whispered. 'You'll draw attention to yourself.'

She reached out with her trunk to comfort the pup.

Then—rustling.

Two more emerged from the bushes. They were adults. LG gasped.

They bared their teeth at her, growling.

LG took a few steps back. 'S-sorry. I was just trying to help. I thought she was lost,' she stammered. Her heart was in her mouth. She remembered Flappy Ears' warning about the wild dholes.

LG turned to flee but froze.

Three more adult dholes had appeared from the dark vegetation. They circled her now, snarling. LG did not know what to do. She was trapped.

Then—like a bolt of lightning from the dark—eight magnificent spotted deer with powerful antlers charged into the circle, sending the dholes scattering in every direction.

This was LG's moment!

She bolted, her feet pounding against the thick undergrowth. Over her shoulders, she caught a glimpse of one of them. LG recognised him instantly. He was one of Killer's friends!

She wanted to thank them, but there was no time.

The forest blurred past as she trundled away from the pack of dholes.

Had she missed the Soul Tree in the melee? She wasn't sure.

But at this moment, only one thing mattered—that she survived.

LG did not stop.

The deeper she went into the jungle, the darker it grew. The scent of delicious leaves tempted her. She remembered the deerberries she had with Killer. They had agreed with her tummy.

Finding fruits in the forest was easy. They were everywhere—elongated green ones that hung from the tops of tall trees, tiny black ones that grew in bunches on short shrubs, red ones on plants double her height. She didn't know what to pick.

Finally, she settled on the small, black ones: they were sour and slightly sweet. Curious, she nibbled on their leaves too. She instantly liked them. She chewed slowly before swallowing, recalling Old Mama's advice to the younger elephants: 'Chew before you swallow,' she would say, marching up and down the pastures as they grazed.

9

THE BUTTERFLY'S KISS

A white butterfly with crimson wing tips fluttered from a plant with yellow flowers and landed on the berry plant. LG noticed it immediately. She was mesmerised by its colours and dropped the berries to run after it.

The butterfly flitted around playfully as LG chased it around. It would slow down just enough to let LG think she could catch it— only to take off as she came close. LG squealed with delight!

She sang:

Dear wings of light, care to offer me a ride?
Let me hold on to your red tip.
Take me up, up, up, till we come upon the
Soul Tree.

LG was now dancing, forgetting all else. In that moment, she felt like a calf again—

carefree with a heart filled with happiness. The butterfly took LG's mind off the weight of her journey. It was a distraction she needed badly. The past two weeks had tested her in ways she had never imagined. But, now, she felt like her old self again.

Lost in thought, LG didn't realise she was following the butterfly.

The butterfly finally landed on her head. It felt so soft, like clouds: the butterfly's kiss. LG smiled.

Then, suddenly, something charged at her from behind.

LG fell on her side, her head hitting a thorny shrub. She felt dizzy. The creature grunted, and LG realised it was standing very close to her. She had to get back on her feet before it made its next move. She forced herself to her feet just in time.

The creature lunged at her, and in the dim light, she caught a glimpse of black stripes on a dirty-brown coat. She felt its powerful claws

strike her trunk. When it pounced on her once again, LG moved swiftly to her side. It missed. LG panted, flaying her trunk in every direction.

She realised what it was: a striped hyena.

In the chaos, something on the ground caught her eye: a broken butterfly wing, white with a red tip. Her friend was crushed in the encounter. LG closed her eyes, gritted her teeth and charged at the hyena, trumpeting like the sound of thunder. She was fuming! She hit the hyena squarely on the side of his stomach. He wailed in pain. LG prepared for another attack, but before that, the hyena limped away, defeated.

LG was relieved that she survived the attack of a full-grown hyena, but what about the butterfly? She had to die for no fault of her own.

How unfair.

LG walked on, her head hanging low. How many other smaller creatures suffered the same fate? Bugs, bees, butterflies, reptiles—

were they not as important as the elephants and tigers?

LG picked a trunkful of earth, looking at the tiny lives within—worms and ants and other tiny wriggling creatures. She did not even know their names. And yet, they were alive. A part of the same world as she was. LG felt no different from them. For the first time, she understood: she was no different from the tiniest bug in the forest, the smallest leaf that lay on the forest floor. The realisation filled her with peace. LG's mind, which was a jumble of thoughts just moments earlier, calmed down. Now, all she felt was a strange sense of lightness.

10

A REUNION AMIDST THE NEELAKURINJI

L G walked at a steady pace, covering long distances effortlessly. The sky was growing lighter. Dawn was breaking over the forest. In the soft glow, she noticed a tree—so tall that it appeared to stretch out into infinity. Its leaves were shaped like stars, and its wide trunk had patches of peeling bark. LG walked up to it.

At the centre of the trunk sat a small yellow butterfly. LG stood very still. More butterflies fluttered in, settling close together in a perfect circle. The tree now appeared to have a beating heart. LG reached out and touched the circle with her trunk. The butterflies scattered. The tree felt warm, and LG closed her eyes. She had arrived at the Soul Tree.

A vision filled her mind—rolling mountain slopes covered in purple-blue neelakurinji flowers. Her mother had told her how Old Mama always took the herd to the slopes to graze on the fertile mountain grass. Neelakurinji bloomed only once in twelve years, and Old Mama had promised to take LG there that year. 'It is a sight worth waiting for,' Old Mama had said.

LG hoped her herd would be somewhere near the flowers. Holding that image in her heart, she placed her trunk on the Soul Tree. She felt nothing at first. Then, the tree took her inside it in a soft embrace and a light—so bright that LG had to shut her eyes—engulfed her. Whooosh.

When LG opened her eyes, she found herself standing in the middle of a field of purple-blue flowers. The neelakurinji stretched as far as the eye could see. The sun was beginning to rise, its golden glow spreading over the flowers, lighting them up little by little. LG held her breath. She had never seen anything so beautiful.

~

'Did I fail my daughter? Am I failing my herd?' Mother was weighed down by so many questions. They seemed to sear her from the inside. She wandered, not knowing where her feet were taking her. Only a miracle would bring back LG. She had heard of elephant camps from Old Mama—was her daughter trapped in one of them? Would she ever see her again?

Oh, my baby, I'm so sorry, sobbed Mother.

She climbed a slope covered in blue flowers. Neelakurinji. Mother had been pregnant with LG the last time she stood there. Old Mama had promised that when the flowers bloomed, she could bring her calf here—to run, to play, to graze to her heart's content.

Mother took a deep breath. She knew she couldn't keep her herd waiting. They had to move on. She had to move on. She squared her shoulders and started walking, determined to gather them before sunset.

Then, something caught her eye. A tiny grey shape on a faraway slope, barely visible through the mist. An elephant! As the mist parted, recognition struck her like lightning.

'LG!' Mother screamed. 'LG!'

A joyous trumpet answered her.

Mother charged through the neelakurinji flowers towards her little girl. She ran and ran, trumpeting along the way.

When she reached LG, she skidded to a halt, panting.

'Mother!' LG exclaimed.

'My baby, my baby,' sobbed Mother, wrapping her daughter in her trunk. They held each other, crying for a long time.

'I'm sorry, LG,' said Mother. 'I should have kept a better watch on you. It's all my fault. I hope you're not hurt. Are you hungry? Do you want to drink milk? Oh LG!' she sobbed.

LG peeled herself from her mother's embrace to talk. She had so much to tell her!

'I have two names now, Mother,' she giggled. 'They also call me Paapa.' She looked up, eyes shining. 'Wait till you hear everything that happened.'

ABOUT THE AUTHOR

Akila Kannadasan is a journalist by day and a writer by night. She has crossed oceans and wandered through forests in search of stories worth telling. Living close to the Western Ghats, she counts herself lucky to be on nodding terms with many tamed elephants—and a few wild ones too. She feels most alive when writing about birds and butterflies, snails and ants, trees and turtles, and spends much of her time in their company. A lover of the sea and its people, she treasures a vast collection of shells kissed by the waves.

AUTHOR'S NOTE

A few years ago, I witnessed the taming of a wild elephant at an elephant camp in the Western Ghats. He had been captured after an agonising operation involving excavators, ropes, trucks and tranquiliser darts. Deemed 'problematic' for entering farmlands and helping himself to produce, he was sentenced to spend the rest of his life as a camp elephant.

When I saw him up close, he stood inside a *kraal*—a wooden enclosure used to break a wild elephant. As I approached, he reached out his trunk, hoping for food. It was heartbreaking to see such a powerful, majestic being reduced to that.

Elephants are among the most fascinating creatures on our planet—gentle giants that trundle through forests in close-knit herds, led by wise matriarchs. Yet today, they make headlines for the wrong reasons: being run over by trains, breaking into homes on forest fringes, and sometimes, trampling humans.

Human–elephant conflict affects both man and animal. Elephants, however, suffer for no fault of theirs. Those deemed a threat to human settlements are captured and brought to elephant camps. One such camp is the Theppakadu Elephant Camp in the Mudumalai Tiger Reserve in the Nilgiris. It has been run by the Tamil Nadu Forest Department for over a century. It was here that I first met abandoned elephant calves who inspired this story—and the mahouts who dedicated their lives to them.

To observe an elephant camp is to witness the heart-warming bond between two completely different species. As soon as an elephant arrives, it is assigned a mahout. These men—often from the Malasar, Kurumba and Kattunayakar tribal communities—stay by their side through the first difficult weeks, even sleeping beside them in the open. Slowly, the elephant begins to trust. The mahout learns his rhythms; the elephant learns his voice.

These men care for their elephants like their own children: waking with them, feeding them huge balls of boiled rice and finger millet, bathing them, talking to them and taking them to the forest to graze. They teach them commands, tend to their wounds and brush neem oil gently onto their toes to prevent infection. Some mahouts never recover from the loss of their elephants. Their eyes well up at even a mention of the one they've lost.

But are camp elephants happy? Do they still dream of the forest?

Recently, an elephant from the camp was taken to help capture another wild elephant—right in the same forest where he had once roamed freely. He was tied to a tree in the very place he had once walked without a care in the world. The operation went smoothly. But we don't know what he felt inside—whether the return to that spot made him feel helpless or heartbroken.

We can only hope that he is at peace, wherever he is.

www.ingramcontent.com/pod-product-compliance
Lightning Source LLC
Chambersburg PA
CBHW060334310726
48976CB00007B/2554